The Poop Song

By **Eric Litwin**

Illustrated by **Claudia Boldt**

chronicle books · san francisco

CATS poop in their own little box.

MOUNTAIN GOATS poop as they climb over rocks.

FISHES poop as they swim in the sea.

CATERPILLARS poop at the top of a tree.

Everybody's pooping all day long.

That's why we sing

the **POOPING SONG.**

Pooping.
Pooping.

Everybody's
pooping.

Everybody's pooping around.

But the **BIG BOYS** and **BIG GIRLS**
are pooping in the potty.

And then we hear a happy sound.

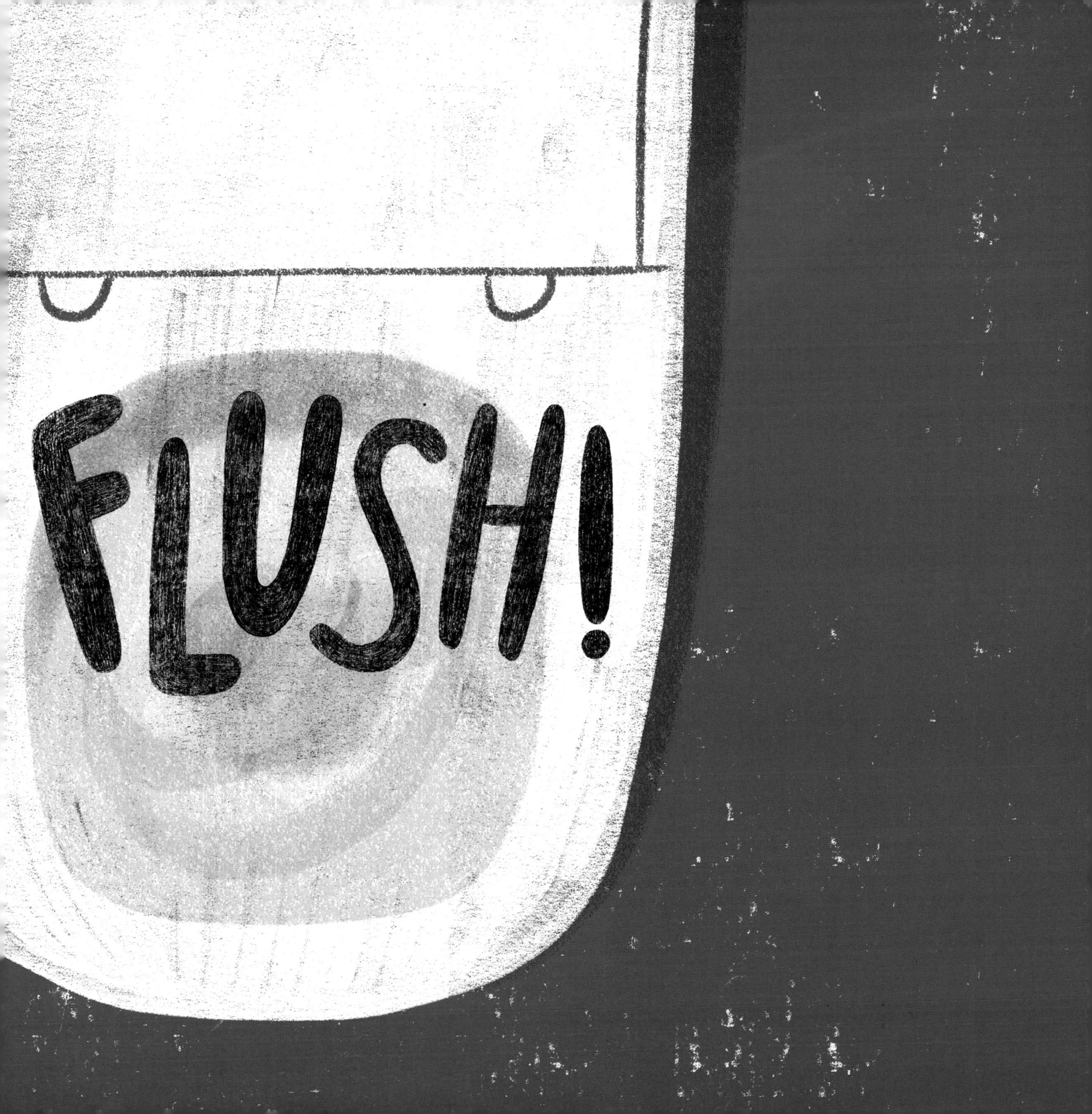
FLUSH!

CAMELS poop in the blazing hot sun.

ELEPHANT poop weighs nearly a ton.

SPACE MARTIANS poop by a faraway star.

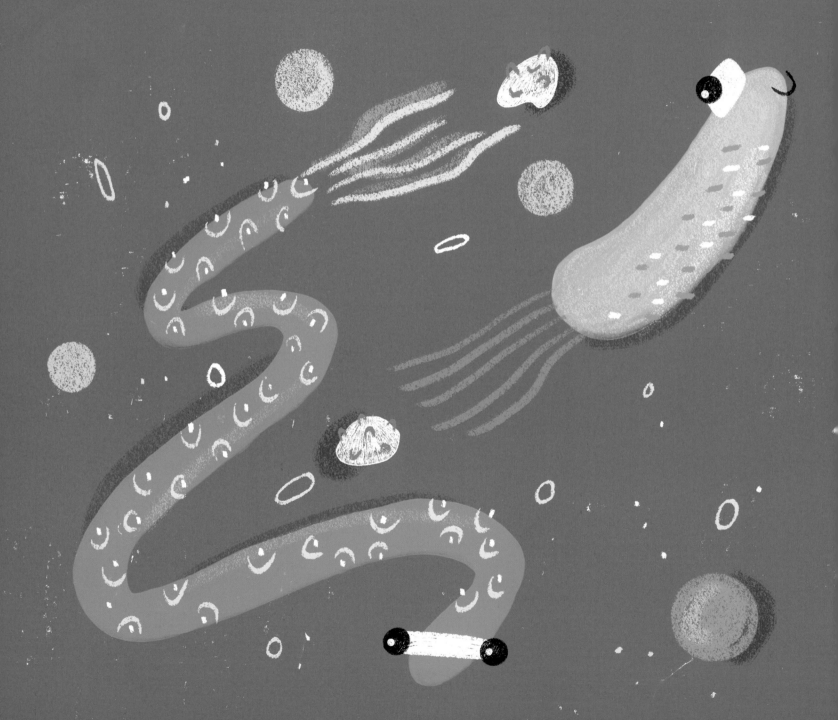

A little **BLUEBIRD** just pooped on my car.

Everybody's pooping all day long.
That's why we sing
the **POOPING SONG.**

Pooping. Pooping.
Everybody's pooping.

Everybody's
pooping around.

But the **BIG BOYS** and **BIG GIRLS**
are pooping in the potty.

And then we hear a happy sound.

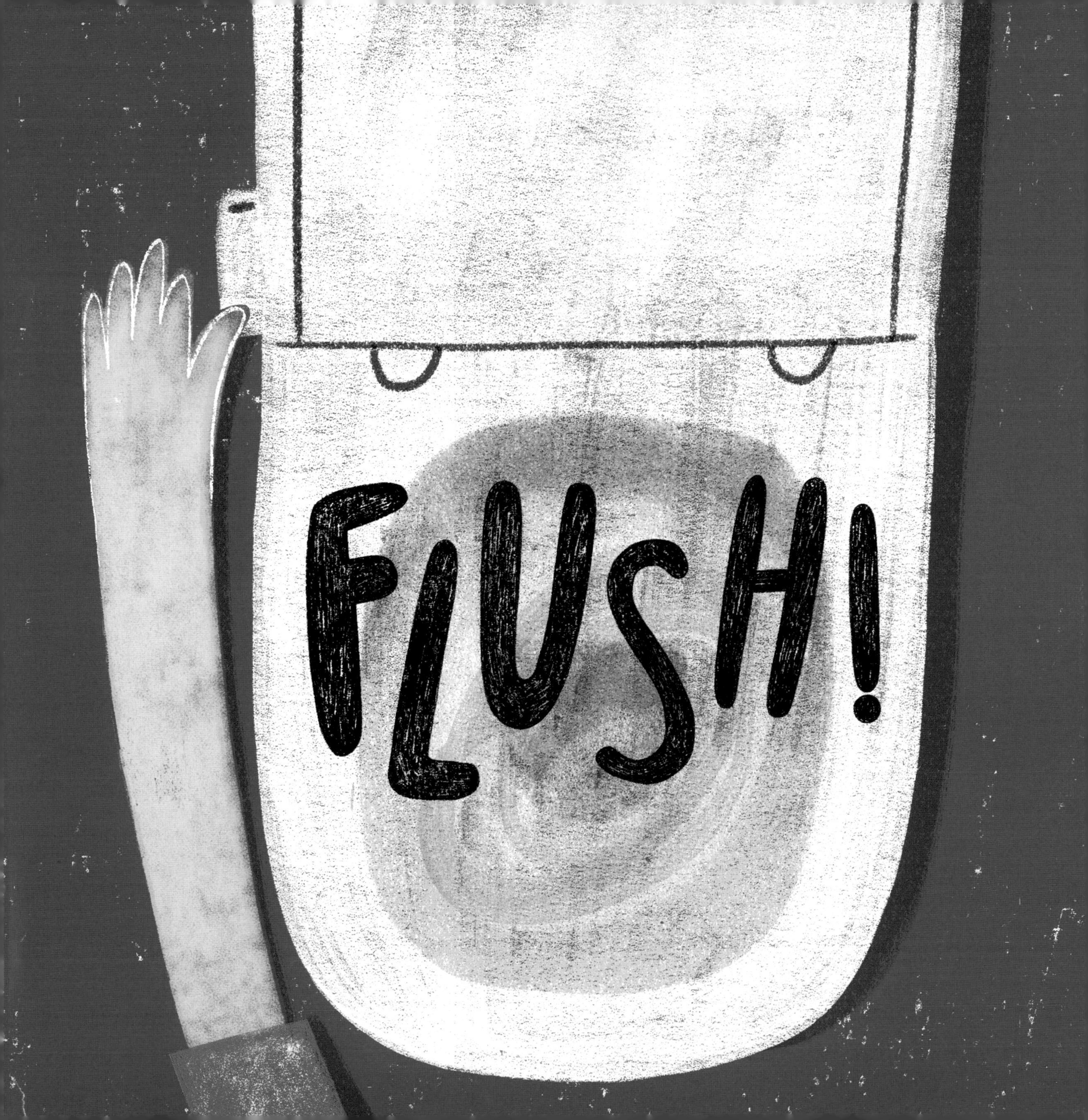
FLUSH!

POLAR BEARS poop in the freezing cold snow.

DINOSAURS pooped a long time ago.

PELICANS poop in a tropical breeze.

BABIES just poop anyplace that they please.

Everybody's pooping all day long.

That's why we sing

the **POOPING SONG.**

But the **BIG BOYS** and **BIG GIRLS** are pooping in the potty.

And then we hear a happy sound.

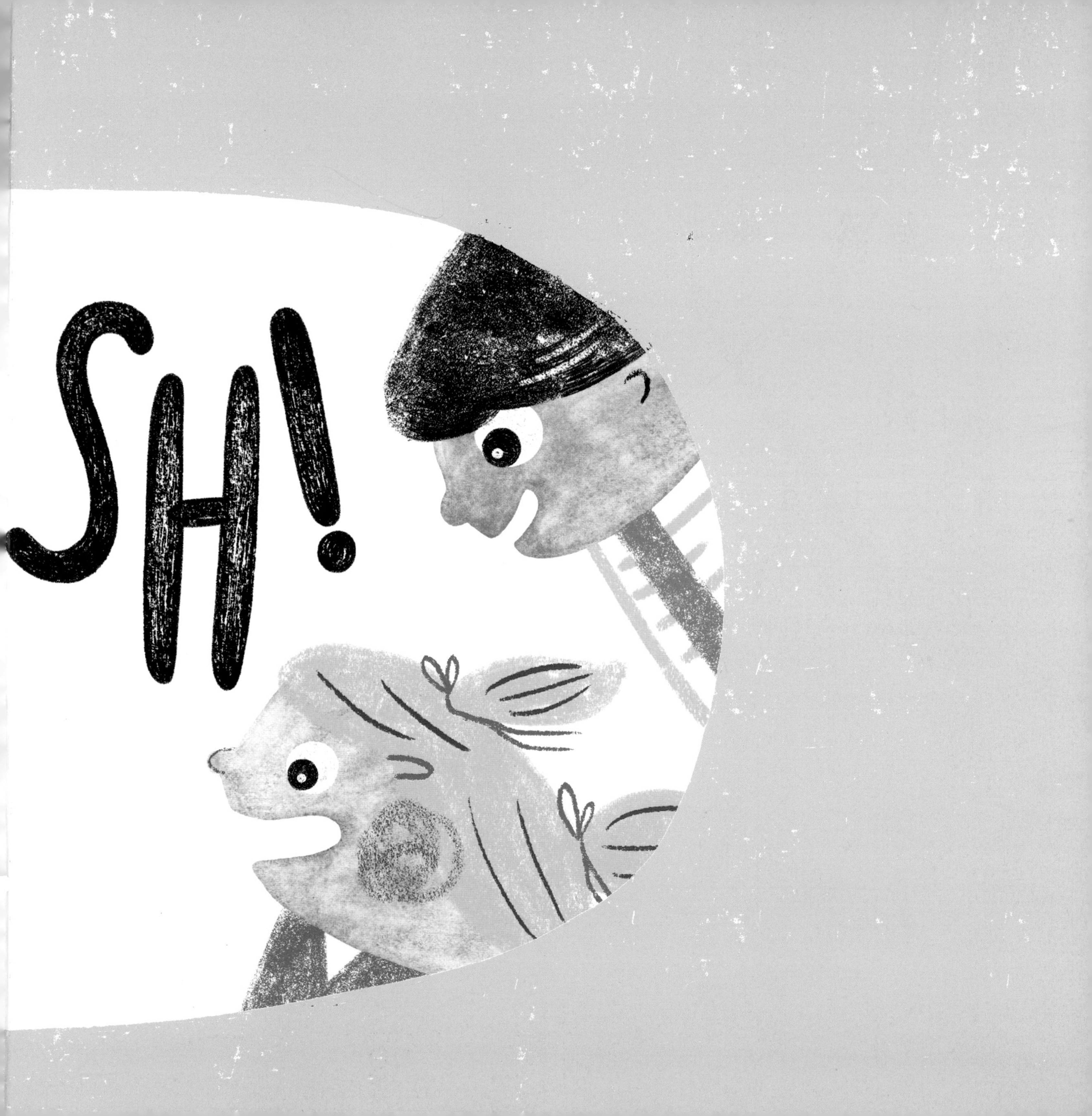
SH!